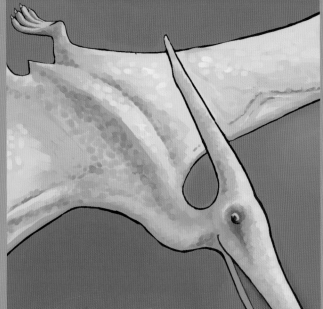

I Am a
Tyrannosaurus

Anna Grossnickle Hines

Tricycle Press
Berkeley

I have a gigantic head
with long, pointy teeth,
and a great loud roar.

I'm a huge,
ferocious hunter.

I am . . .

a tyrannosaurus.

I'm not so big,
with a stiff tail
and little wings,

but I run fast
and leap, leap, leap.

I am . . .

a velociraptor.

I clomp along
because I'm so big,
with a *looong* tail.

My neck reaches
way, way up
to eat the leaves.

I am . . .

a brachiosaurus.

I have a big collar,
and three horns
on my face.

I look mean,
but I eat only plants.

I am . . .

a triceratops.

My pointy head
has a crest on top
and a beak at the bottom.

I fly and swoop
to scoop up fish.

I am . . .

a pteranodon.

I am curled up—
Tap! Tap! Tap!—
inside a shell.

Peck! Peck! Peck!
Push and stretch.
Crack!

I am . . .

a brand new baby dinosaur.

My mother
watches over me

and brings me
food to eat.

Her name is . . .

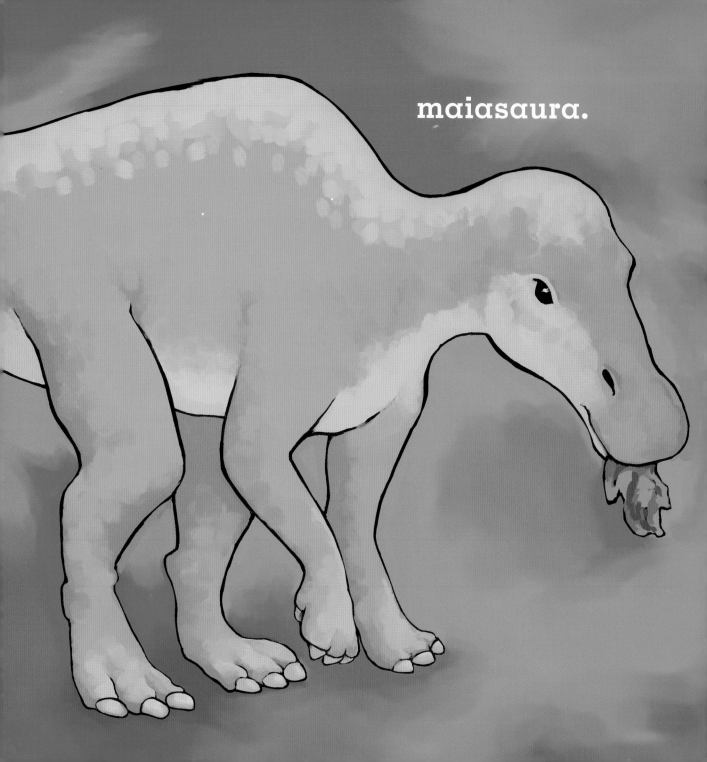

maiasaura.

That means . . .

good mother lizard.

To all the kids who played dinosaur for me:
Landen and Jack, Rowan and Spencer, Pacho and Giovanni,
Henry and Kate, and Ben and Sam

Library of Congress
Cataloging-in-Publication Data
Hines, Anna Grossnickle.
I am a Tyrannosaurus / by Anna Grossnickle Hines. —
1st ed.
p. cm.
Summary: A boy mimics the actions of several
different dinosaurs as he imagines he is one of them.
[1. Dinosaurs—Fiction. 2. Imagination—Fiction.]
I. Title.
PZ7.H572Iat 2011
[E]—dc22
2010024181

ISBN 978-1-58246-413-8 (hardcover)
ISBN 978-1-58246-414-5 (Gibraltar lib. bdg.)

Printed in China

Design by Chloe Rawlins
The illustrations in this book were created digitally.
Typeset in Memphis

1 2 3 4 5 6 – 16 15 14 13 12 11

First Edition

Velociraptor
(veh-lah-si-rap-ter)
"speedy robber"

Pteranodon
(tare-on-uh-don)
"winged toothless"

Brachiosaurus
(bra-key-oh-sore-us)
"arm lizard"

Maiasaura
(my-uh-sore-uh)
"good mother lizard"

Triceratops
(try-ser-uh-tops)
"three-horn face"

Tyrannosaurus
(tie-ran-uh-sore-us)
"tyrant lizard king"

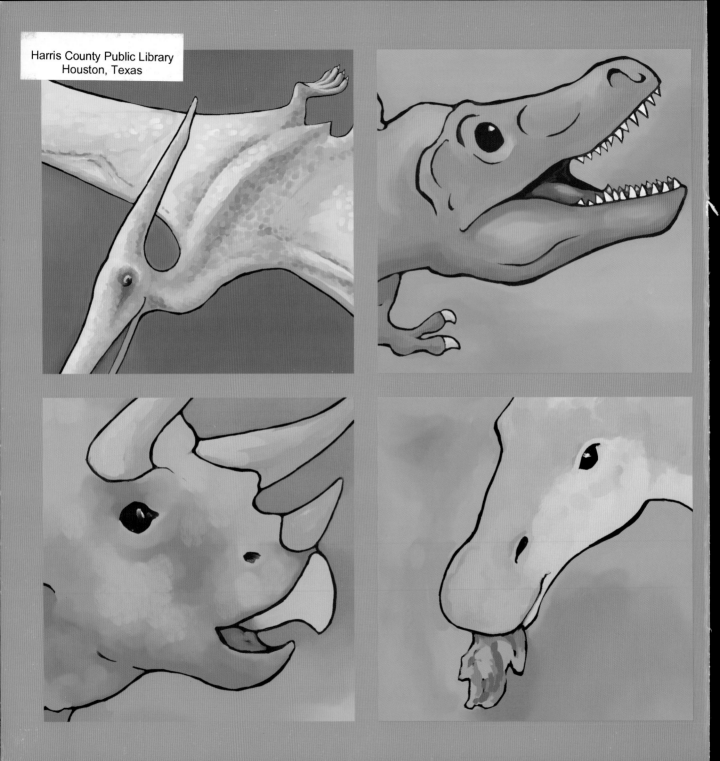